T0197542

Scotty the Scotch Pine

Written and created by
Joyce L. Platt

To order additional copies of this book, contact:
Xlibris
844-714-8691
www.Xlibris.com
Orders@Xlibris.com

ISBN: Softcover   978-1-6698-4436-5
         Hardcover   978-1-6698-4437-2
         EBook   978-1-6698-4435-8

Library of Congress Control Number: 2022915832

Print information available on the last page

Rev. date: 11/04/2022

This story is dedicated to

Melissa, the Crafter, 1973-2020
Carisa, the Namer
Thomas, the Woodcrafter

The little Scotch pine tree wondered why his quiet evergreen forest was now noisy with people. They were wandering about touching his branches, looking serious and talking excitedly. A father watched his two little girls and his boy jump up and down.

They pointed to the little tree and cheered, "Let's get this one!"

1

Before the little tree knew it, he was on the back of a pickup truck zooming down the highway. He stared at the only home he ever knew, as it grew smaller in the distance.

2

The little tree was troubled but remained brave. He wondered what was happening to him. Who are these people? Where were they taking him? He became even more anxious when he was taken off the truck and carried into a house. He had never been in a house and wondered why he was not outside where trees belong. Desperately, he wished he could RUN back to his safe evergreen forest.

The father cried, "Ouch!" when he got poked with sharp needles, but he continued to put the tree in front of a big window.

"At least I can see outside," thought the little tree. "Oh, I see more trees like me in the windows of houses across the street." Puzzled, he scratched his bark.

6

The Green family fluffed the tree's branches, positioned him to stand tall, and smiled at him a lot. Next thing he knew, the father was wrapping him with strings of colored lights. Mr. Green struggled and yelled 'ouch' a lot, as the tree tried to defend himself. The tree was afraid of what they might do next. He had never known of a tree to wear objects. How ridiculous! Then he noticed trees in neighborhood windows covered with lights and decorations.

He saw little shining balls, popcorn strings, silver garland and tinsel, cranberries, and gingerbread cookies. Each tree looked different though somewhat the same. They appeared to be safe in their houses. In fact, some were standing proudly as though in a competitive fashion show. Some had stars or angels on their tops. One wore a big red bow.

Then, the little tree thought, "Well, since those trees don't look scared maybe I should relax."

Neighborhood trees

9

10

The children had worked for weeks making ornaments for their new Christmas tree. Baby Dumpling liked to use items some people would throw away, like fabric scraps, buttons, yarn, paper, sticks, and things from her mother's sewing basket. She made little teddy bears from old nylon stockings stuffed with cotton. She made angels with foil wings and pipe cleaner elves with little felt hats.

Her beaded strings sparkled in the glow of the colored lights. Proudly, she hung all of her treasures on the tree. Near the tree, she gently placed her very special nativity set. She had formed the Holy Family with cone - shaped paper bodies covered with fabric, stick arms, and cotton – stuffed nylon heads. Kind faces were painted on each one. Yarn made fine hair. Watching over the baby Jesus was two angels, two shepherds, and three wise men.

Baby Dumpling's nativity set.

13

Baby Dolly made cookies in the shape of gingerbread children, trees, and mittens. Special names were on each one. Sometimes it was a nickname. Her gift for naming showed as she hung them on the tree.

The family gave all the extra cookies to the birds.

Baby Darlin' enjoyed woodworking. He used wood scraps from his father's woodpile, clothespins, and popsicle sticks. His toy trains, sleds, and soldiers found special spots on the tree.

Mother added some finishing touches like little glass balls and silver garland. She also watered it daily so it would stay nice and green.

15

Traditionally, the family lit the lights, clapped their hands, and awesomely admired the tree. The little tree hoped the decorations would not fall off if he jiggled his branches. He did not understand the importance of looking glamorous, but since the family treated him gently, he did not mind them touching him anymore.

Then Mother gently sang, "Chestnuts roasting on an open fire..."

16

17

Father carefully placed the special tree topper.

The tree got used to guests admiring his decorations. Ladies would affectionately pinch a branch and say, "Isn't he cute?" Mysterious pretty packages appeared under his branches. Sometimes he missed his Evergreen Forest friends, but his branches relaxed and he was less afraid. Whenever the children passed by, they would pause and smile at him.

After weeks of anticipation, Christmas day came. Family gifts were unwrapped, and cheer filled the house. That is when the proud tree shined his brightest. He felt very warm and cozy.

A week after Christmas the little tree felt disturbed as he looked out the window. Many neighborhood trees were now bare. He gasped when he saw their needles falling as they were dragged across the snow. They resembled skeletons on the curb! The little tree was so horrified he felt like petrified wood. Would the Greens who loved him do such a thing? Would he be thrown to the curb, too? Trembling, he nervously dropped some needles to the floor.

Things only looked worse. CHUCKY THE WOODCHUCKER, a monster truck making grinding and screeching noises, was picking up trees. In one end went a dead tree and out the other end came wood chips.

22

It was enough to scare any tree. He bravely stood up straight while trying to look his best. Chills went up and down his trunk. He could not move a branch. "The Greens might throw me out if I look bare and ugly," thought the little tree, "I must hold on to my needles." Mother carefully removed the treasured ornaments and boxed them for next Christmas. Surprised, he heard father say, "It is time to take the tree outside."

The little tree felt bare and frightened.
Prayers poured through his folded raised
branches.

Sad, sticky sap tears streamed from
his top branch all the way down to the
bottom of his trunk.

Mr. Green did not take the tree to the curb. Gently he carried the little tree to the backyard. He placed its roots into a hole and patted soft dirt around its trunk. Baby Dolly named him SCOTTY. Father christened him. Baby Darlin' made Scotty a wood sign with his name on it.

Scotty wiggled his relaxed roots deep into the soft earth. Happy and relieved, he adjusted himself to stand straight and tall. He joyfully raised his branches toward the shining sun.

Close enough to almost touch, Scotty noticed another evergreen tree. A small wood sign read "Piney the White Pine." With glee, she welcomed Scotty. "I have been waiting a whole year for you," she cheered. Immediately, they became friends.

Piney told Scotty about her exciting backyard life. Through the seasons, she had watched the Green family plant, grow, and harvest a garden. Baby Dolly coated Piney's pinecones with peanut butter and homegrown sunflower seeds. The winter birds loved them.

Baby Darlin' made a birdhouse. Mother kept Piney watered and Father wrapped her in colored lights for Christmas. It was a wonderful life.

The Green's house and yard.

Scotty loved hearing Piney's stories. He no longer yearned for the evergreen forest. He felt at home with his new Ever Green family. The next Christmas Mr. Green was not poked when he covered the two outdoor trees with lights.

A year later, a new Christmas tree came out of the back door. Douglas Fir was planted next to Scotty. Remembering how nervous he felt last year, Scotty kindly welcomed Douglas. This threesome was the beginning of a long grove of transplanted Christmas trees. The children made name signs for each one.

The new Green forest included Fraser Fir, Bruce Spruce, Whitey Pine, Sam Balsam, and Blues Spruce.

"Scott and Piney sitting in the back"

Piney   Skott

People are planting the tree.

Merry Christmas

Happy Birthday

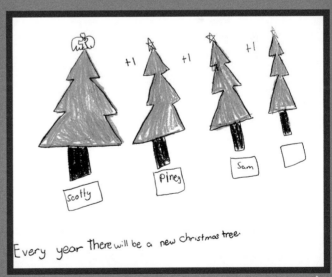

+1   +1   +1

Scotty   Piney   Sam

Every year there will be a new christmas tree.

As they grew taller their branches grew wider and they protected the house from the winter winds. The trees never felt the cold because their branches were always touching each other.

33

Many years later- Ever GREEN Family

Credits and Crumbs

ILLUSTRATIONS: By children to whom I have read the story. Special thanks to the children of Saipan who gifted their original drawings to me.

PHOTOGRAPHS:
P. 13 Melissa's Nativity Set
P. 34 Metty Meadows by Niece Monica

Their branches were always touching each other.

Printed in the United States
by Baker & Taylor Publisher Services